RIVER TOWN

 HOUGHTON MIFFLIN

BOSTON

Printed in Mexico   ISBN 10: 0-547-00736-1   123456789-RDT-13 12 11 10 09 08 07
                           ISBN 13: 978-0-547-00736-6

CAST OF CHARACTERS

Narrator

Mr. Sharp storekeeper

Mrs. Sharp storekeeper

Rob Sharp son

Emma Sharp daughter

Mrs. Hall English traveler

Sam Moore farmer

Boatman flatboat pilot

Captain steamboat captain

And featuring The Bells and Whistles **Band**

Setting: General Store in Otters Landing, Summer day, 1826.

Narrator The river where Emma Sharp lives is like a highway. People, goods, and news are carried from place to place. Today is Emma's birthday, and she wishes for something only the river can bring. But today is busier than usual at her family's store and inn. Very busy.

(A bell jingles over the front door of the general store as Mrs. Hall enters.)

Mr. Sharp Morning, Mrs. Hall!

Mrs. Hall Good morning, Mr. Sharp.

Mr. Sharp I trust you slept well at the inn?

Mrs. Hall Yes, thank you. It was delightful… if you don't mind bedbugs.

Mr. Sharp Happy to hear it, ma'am. Can I get you something?

Mrs. Hall Yes. I was hoping—

(Bell over the door jingles.)

Emma *(excited)* Father! A flatboat's coming down the river! It's a big one.

Mrs. Sharp Emma! Mind your manners.

Emma Oh, sorry. *(to Mrs. Hall)* Pardon me, ma'am… Father, may I go watch it dock? I finished with the sweeping.

Rob Can I go too? The wood is all stacked.

Emma Please, Father.

Mr. Sharp Go ahead then, but don't get underfoot.

Mrs. Sharp And come right back. There's still much to do here.

Rob I'll see if anyone needs help, and then we'll be back.

(Jingle of door bell as Rob and Emma leave.)

Mrs. Hall *(clears throat loudly)* As I was saying, I wondered if you have something for—

(Jingle of door bell.)

Sam Moore Good morning! *(nods to Mrs. Hall)* Ma'am.

Mr. Sharp and **Mrs. Sharp** Hello, Sam.

Sam Moore My list is short today. *(reciting from memory)* Nails, molasses, coffee, a packet of needles, pie pan, pitcher, salt, new comb—Sally stepped on her favorite one, and she's beside herself—stick of licorice if you've got some. Beeswax. Did I say that?

Narrator That's a short list? Well, yes, for Sam. No matter how long it is, Sam always adds in the licorice, and Mr. Sharp always says the same thing.

Mr. Sharp My word, Samuel Moore. Is it your birthday? It's not? Well, then, what have you got to trade?

Sam Moore Corn, butter, eggs… Look in my wagon.

(Jingle of door bell as they leave.)

Mrs. Hall Now, Mrs. Sharp, if you please, I need something for—

(Door bell jingles as door swings open.)

Mr. Sharp Sam's got feathers. Can we use feathers?

Mrs. Sharp Yes! For that old bed at the inn.

(Bell jingles as door shuts.)

Mrs. Hall *(yells)* —for the bedbugs! Oh, I'm itchy! *(quietly)* IF you don't mind.

Mrs. Sharp Of course. Skeeters are pesky this season, too, aren't they? Here is some witch hazel. Made it up myself. Very soothing. Today is Emma's birthday, not Mr. Moore's. That's bit of a joke. *(to herself)* Ooo, low on molasses...

Narrator While the Sharps are busy in the store, the flatboat approaches the landing. The men on board use large oars to bring it in, and Rob helps them tie it up.

Boatman Thank you, friend.

Rob Not at all. How was your trip?

Boatman That storm last week made a mess. We hit a big snag below Hillsville. Trees down in the river. Hope it's better between here and the city. We've got corn from up the river to go to market.

Rob Up at the store, my father will have some goods for you.

Boatman We also brought the Hawkins family downriver. Six, all told.

Rob Where are they from?

Boatman East of Hillsville, heading somewhere. Not settling here at Otters Landing. Somewhere south. They'll be on foot, hoping to hitch a ride. Imagine they're worried.

(Rob motions to Emma to join them.)

Rob *(to Emma)* Wasn't that Sam Moore's wagon up at the store?

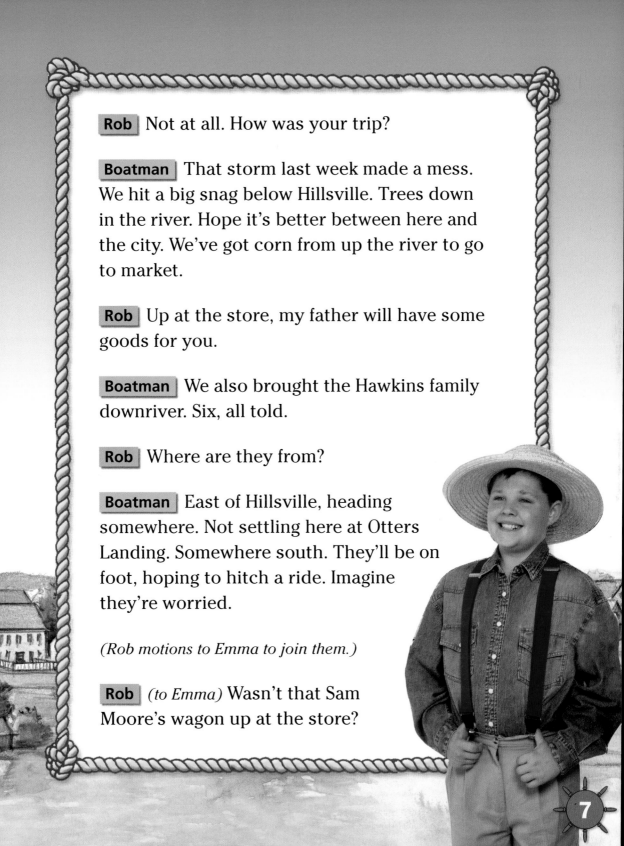

7

Emma Yes, I saw it coming in.

Rob *(to the boatman)* He lives out past Roundtop. He might give them a ride.

Emma He'd walk the whole way to help somebody out.

Narrator Rob and Emma watch the activity on the flatboat as the flatboat pilot talks to the Hawkins family. A group leaves the dock and heads to the store. Emma doesn't look very happy.

Rob Emma? What's the matter? They'll be fine.

Emma I want to stay here and wait for the steamboat.

Rob But we need you at the store.

Emma It was supposed to come two days ago! And it hasn't come yet.

Rob I know. That's why Mrs. Hall and those other English people are still here.

Emma I love the steamboat whistle. I haven't heard it since I was nine.

Rob I see, and now you're ancient. Ten?

Emma You know I am.

Rob I thought you were worried about that family... Well, you know what Mother says: a watched pot never boils. Let's go back. We have chores to do.

Emma I just like the big sound... the way it bounces off the water. Makes my hair stand up.

Rob Is that what does it? Well, we should— Look! *(points)* A trading boat, coming upriver!

Emma *(pointing in the opposite direction)* Rob! Look over there.

Rob Another flatboat. Let's go tell Father. Maybe we can get back to watch them come in.

Narrator They race to the store, and Rob lets Emma win. Two more wagons are tied up in front. The Hawkins family looks a little weary and are talking about a rest at the inn. It's busy inside the store, so Rob and Emma have to stay and help.

Mrs. Sharp *(to a customer)* This sturdy cloth will make good work pants… How much do you need?

Mr. Sharp *(to another customer)* The roads are better from here to the city, weather permitting.

Rob *(to a farmer)* Five bushels of beans. Yes sir. We can send those to market. This morning's flatboat will be going out soon.

Sam Moore *(to Mrs. Hall)* Think I'll stay a while. See what the boats bring in. Never seen it like this. Mighty quiet where I live.

Mrs. Hall When will the STEAMboat arrive? Does anyone know? We have been waiting days. Days.

Mrs. Sharp Maybe they had engine trouble. Steam engines are tricky. Sometimes they blow sky high.

Sam Moore They say you should sit as far from the engine as possible. Just in case.

Mrs. Hall *(faintly)* Oh dear.

(Jingle of door bell. Flatboat pilot enters.)

Boatman I'm ready to start loading.

Mr. Sharp Good. We've got beans, too. Let's step outside. Rob, I'll need your help.

(Jingle of door bell as they leave.)

Narrator It's late in the day. Time has passed quickly for everyone but Emma and Mrs. Hall.

Mrs. Hall This is pure tedium, I say. We must find another way to get to Hillsville. Mr. Sharp, is there a carriage for hire?

Mr. Sharp The stagecoach gallops through with the mail tomorrow. No carriages otherwise, ma'am.

Emma I was so much wishing to hear that whistle today. *(sigh)*

Mrs. Sharp Cheer up, Emma. We'll have a party with the neighbors after supper. I made your favorite jam cakes.

Emma *(sadly)* I know.

(Silence. Then… a whistle starts low and quiet; slowly slides up to a long loud high note; the high note repeats.)

Band Ooooooooooooooooooooooooh! Ooooooh! Oooooooh!

Emma *(gasps)* It's the steamboat! It's coming!

Mrs. Hall Gracious!

Band Ooooooooooooooooh! Oooooooooh!

Emma *(shouting)* Listen! Listen! The steamboat! Listen!

Mr. Sharp How can we, with you carrying on?

Rob Let's go!

Mrs. Hall Yes. Yes!

Band Jingle, jingle, jingle!

Narrator When the steamboat docks, everyone, all of the Otters Landing townspeople, watch as the gangplank is laid between the riverbank and the boat. Passengers get off. Freight is unloaded. The Sharps talk with the steamboat captain.

Mrs. Sharp Hello, Captain. You have quite a haul.

Captain Yes, indeed. Several families, plus household goods and livestock. Some are settling near here. They'll want supplies.

Mr. Sharp I know just where they can get them.

Mrs. Hall Excuse me, Captain. I'm Mrs. Hall. What has kept you?

Captain Mechanical difficulties, ma'am. We're fine now. Just don't let me go over three miles an hour!

Mrs. Hall Oh no…

Mrs. Sharp *(to the Captain)* When will you be back down this way?

Captain In about a week. I'll have hogs and wheat and whatnot. We'll do business then. *(pauses)* Mrs. Hall, I advise you to get yourself aboard if you're coming.

Emma Captain! Captain!

Captain Hello, Miss Emma. Haven't seen you in a long while.

Emma Guess what day it is. Guess what day.

Captain Thursday, last I heard.

Emma Guess again.

Captain The day the boat was late, once more, because the captain was stumped by the questions of—

Emma It's my birthday.

Captain Is that so? Well, now. What might you want for your birthday. Let me think. It's coming back to me now...

Narrator When the steamboat chugs very slowly away from Otters Landing, Mrs. Hall is safely on board. Oh. She did come to appreciate Mrs. Sharp's itch remedy and she said so, kindly. Look. The Sharps and the townspeople are waving good-bye from the riverbank.

Emma *(signaling the captain)* Now!

Band Oooooooooooooooooooooooh! Ooooooooh! Ooooooooooh!

GLOSSARY

downriver the direction a river flows

flatboat a flat-bottom boat for carrying heavy loads on slow-moving waterways

gangplank a board or ramp used as a walkway between a boat and dock

stagecoach horse-drawn carriage that makes short, fast trips

tedium something that is boring

upriver the opposite direction of a river's flow

witch hazel a soothing lotion made from the plant of the same name